Contents

"BEYOND THE HORIZON: A JOURNEY OF SCIENTIFIC DISCOVERY"

MANEET NAGAMALLA

Made with ♥ on the Notion Press Platform
www.notionpress.com

CHAPTER ONE

"The Discovery"

The lab was abuzz with excitement. Rd. Elizabeth Reynolds paced around the room; her eyes fixed on the computer screen displaying the results of the latest experiment.

"We did it!" she exclaimed. "We've successfully built a time machine!"

Her team erupted in cheers and applause. After years of research and development, they had finally achieved their goal. The machine was small and unassuming, but it held the power to transport them through time.

As the team gathered around the machine, Rd. Reynolds couldn't help but feel a sense of awe. She had always been fascinated by the idea of time travel but had never truly believed it was possible. And yet, here they were, on the cusp of an incredible discovery.

The team spent the next few hours testing the machine. They sent small objects through time, marvelling as they appeared in a different era. It was a surreal experience, knowing that they were manipulating time itself.

As night fell, the team decided to take a risk and test the machine on themselves. Rd. Reynolds volunteered to go first, strapping herself into the machine and setting the controls for 1920.

She closed her eyes as the machine whirred to life. When she opened them again, she was standing in the middle of a bustling New York City Street. The buildings were shorter, the cars were boxier, and the people were dressed in outdated fashions. But it was undeniably 1920.

Rd. Reynolds couldn't contain her excitement. She ran up to a passer-by and asked what year it was, barely able to keep the glee out of her voice. When the man replied, she whooped with joy. It had worked!

As she explored the city, Rd. Reynolds couldn't help but notice the differences between the past and the present. It was like stepping into a different world. She marvelled at the architecture, the clothing, the way of life.

But as the night wore on, she began to realize that their discovery came with a great responsibility. Even the slightest change to the past could have dire consequences for the present. She shuddered at the thought of inadvertently altering history and causing irreparable damage to the timeline.

When the team regrouped the next morning, they were all beaming with excitement. They had just taken the first step towards a new frontier of science. But they also knew that they had to proceed with caution. They had no idea what lay ahead on their journey through time, but they were ready to face it together.

Rd. Reynolds looked around at her team, feeling a sense of pride and camaraderie. They had achieved something incredible, something that would change the course of history. She could hardly wait to see where their invention would take them next.

CHAPTER TWO

"The Butterfly Effect"

As the team continued to explore the past, they quickly discovered that even the smallest actions could have major consequences on the present. They had to be careful not to change anything significant, or risk altering history in ways they couldn't imagine.

The team decided to start small, observing historical events without interfering. They travelled to different time periods, taking in the sights and sounds of the past. They saw the rise and fall of empires, the birth of new technologies, and the struggles of everyday people throughout history.

But as they spent more time in the past, the team began to notice small changes in the present. At first, it was minor things - a book that was once red was now blue, a street that used to be two-way was now one-way. But as they dug deeper, they realized that these changes were signs of a much bigger problem.

One of the team members, Rd. Samuel Chen, had always been fascinated by the idea of the butterfly effect - the concept that a small action in the past could have far-reaching consequences in the present. He started to suspect that the team's actions were causing ripples in time, and that those ripples were growing larger by the day.

The team decided to conduct an experiment to test this theory. They travelled back to the 1800s and observed a group of workers building a bridge. They watched as one of the workers accidentally dropped a tool into the water, causing a small splash. Then they returned to the present day to see what had changed.

To their horror, they discovered that the entire course of history had been altered. The bridge had collapsed during construction, killing hundreds of workers and leading to a major shift in the economy of the region. The effects had rippled outwards, causing a chain reaction of changes throughout the timeline.

The team was devastated. They had never intended to cause harm, but their actions had led to a tragedy of epic proportions. They realized that they had to be even more careful in their travels, and that they couldn't take anything for granted.

Rd. Reynolds and Rd. Chen spent hours poring over historical records, trying to understand the extent of the damage they had caused. They realized that their actions had altered the course of countless lives, and that they couldn't simply undo what they had done.

As they continued to explore the past, the team became more and more aware of the impact of their actions. They started to see their surroundings in a different light - not as a mere backdrop for their travels, but as a living, breathing world that they were responsible for preserving.

One day, while observing the American Civil War, the team witnessed a young girl being injured by a stray bullet. Rd. Reynolds immediately rushed to her aid, administering first aid and saving her life. As she tended to the girl, she realized the importance of their work. They couldn't simply observe history - they had to actively protect it.

From that moment on, the team vowed to be more responsible in their travels. They developed strict protocols for their time travel experiments, including limits on how far back they could go and strict rules against interfering with major historical events.

The team continued to travel through time, but now they did so with a newfound sense of purpose. They weren't just observers - they were guardians of history. And as they journeyed through the past, they worked to ensure that their actions didn't cause harm to the world around them.

Despite their newfound caution, the team knew that they still had a long way to go. The butterfly effect was a powerful force, and they couldn't predict what the future held. But they were determined to be as careful as possible, knowing that the fate of the world was in their hands.

CHAPTER THREE

Chapter 3: "The Temporal Paradox"

The team had been traveling through time for several months, and despite their new protocols, they still encountered unforeseen challenges. On one trip to the year 1945, they discovered that their time machine had malfunctioned, leaving them stranded in the past.

The team was now stuck in the waning days of World War II, in a time and place that they were not meant to be. They had to find a way to repair their time machine and return to their own time before they caused any further damage to the timeline.

Rd. Reynolds, Rd. Chen, and the rest of the team set to work on repairing the time machine. It was a daunting task, as they were working with technology that was decades beyond their own time. They scoured the city, searching for the parts they needed, and working tirelessly day and night to make the necessary repairs.

As they worked, they also had to be careful not to reveal their true identities. They had to blend in with the locals, pretending to be tourists who had been caught up in the war. They knew that even a small slip-up could have disastrous consequences.

Days turned into weeks, and still, the team had not been able to repair the time machine. They were running out of options and resources, and tensions were running high. Rd. Reynolds, who had always been the voice of reason in the team, was becoming increasingly frustrated.

One day, as they were scavenging for parts in a nearby junkyard, they stumbled upon a strange device. It looked like some kind of temporal accelerator - a device that could speed up time. Rd. Chen recognized it immediately and realized that it could be the key to repairing their time machine.

Rd. Chen and the team worked on reverse engineering the device, taking it apart piece by piece and analysing how it worked. It was a difficult process, as they were working with technology that they had never seen before. But after many long hours, they finally figured out how to use the device to repair their time machine.

As they activated the temporal accelerator, the world around them began to blur and distort. They could feel time speeding up, and they knew that they were about to enter a new reality. But as the device reached its peak power, something strange happened.

The team found themselves transported to a new reality - one that was vastly different from the one they had left behind. They were still in 1945, but the world around them was completely changed. The war had ended much sooner than it had in their original timeline, and the world was a much different place.

Rd. Reynolds and the team quickly realized that they had caused a temporal paradox. By using the temporal accelerator, they had altered the timeline in ways they couldn't have predicted. They had inadvertently changed history, and now they had to deal with the consequences.

The team was disoriented and confused, but they knew that they had to act quickly. They had to find a way to reverse the changes they had caused and restore the timeline to its original state. But they quickly realized that it wouldn't be easy - they had altered history in ways they couldn't imagine.

As they began to explore this new reality, the team discovered that the changes they had caused had far-reaching consequences. The war had ended differently, and the world was a vastly different place. There were new technologies, new governments, and new power structures. The team had caused a ripple in time that they couldn't easily undo.

Rd. Reynolds and Rd. Chen were distraught. They had always understood the risks of time travel, but they had never imagined that their actions could have such catastrophic consequences. They knew that they had to find a way to fix their mistake, but they didn't know where

CHAPTER FOUR

"A World Turned Upside Down"

As the team explored the new reality they had created, they couldn't help but feel a sense of awe and unease. The world they had known no longer existed, and they were now in a place that was both familiar and foreign.

Gone were the familiar landmarks and buildings they had grown accustomed to. The skyline was different, the streets were unfamiliar, and even the air felt different. It was like they were in a different country, but they knew they were still in the same place.

The team quickly realized that they were in a world where the outcome of World War II had been drastically altered. Instead of the Allies emerging victorious, the Axis powers had won the war. It was a world turned upside down, and the team had to find a way to make things right.

Rd. Reynolds and Rd. Chen led the team as they searched for a way to undo the changes they had caused. They knew that they had to find the source of the temporal paradox and reverse it before it was too late.

As they walked through the unfamiliar streets, they saw the remnants of a different world. The signs and posters were all in German, and the people around them spoke a language they couldn't understand. The team had to adapt quickly and learn to blend in with the locals.

They eventually made their way to what appeared to be a government building. It was heavily guarded, and they knew they had to be careful. They snuck in and began to search for any information that could help them undo the temporal paradox.

They eventually found a room filled with strange equipment and documents. It appeared to be a research facility, and the team knew that they had found what they were looking for. They began to study the documents, looking for any information that could help them undo the changes they had caused.

It was a difficult task, as the documents were all in German. But with the help of some translation software, they were able to piece together a startling discovery. The research facility they had stumbled upon was working on a project to alter history. They were trying to change the outcome of the war in their Favor, and they had succeeded.

The team was horrified. They had unwittingly stumbled upon a group of time travellers who were working to alter the course of history. They had caused a temporal paradox that had allowed this group to succeed, and they knew they had to put an end to it.

Rd. Reynolds and Rd. Chen devised a plan to destroy the research facility and stop the group from altering history any further. They knew it was a risky move, but it was their only chance to make things right.

They snuck into the facility and set explosives at strategic points. As they made their escape, they triggered the explosives, causing the entire building to collapse. It was a daring move, but it had worked. The research facility was destroyed, and the group responsible for the temporal paradox was no more.

As they made their way back to their time machine, the team knew that they had succeeded in their mission. They had put an end to the temporal paradox they had caused and restored the timeline to its original state. But they also knew that they had learned a valuable lesson - that the consequences of time travel could be far-reaching and unpredictable.

Rd. Reynolds and Rd. Chen knew that they had to be more careful in the future. They had to be sure that they understood the full consequences of their actions before they made any more jumps through time. The team boarded their time machine, set the coordinates for their own time, and began the journey home. They knew that they had a lot to discuss and plan for in the days ahead, but for now, they were just happy to be going back to a familiar world.

CHAPTER FIVE

"The Consequences of Time Travel"

As the team travelled back to their own time, they knew that they had a lot to discuss. They had just experienced the consequences of time travel first-hand, and they had seen the damage that could be caused by a simple mistake. Rd. Reynolds and Rd. Chen knew that they had to be more careful in the future, and they knew that they had to take some time to reflect on what they had learned.

When they arrived back in their own time, they were met by their colleagues and a team of government officials. The officials were concerned about the consequences of their experiment and wanted to know more about what had happened. Rd. Reynolds and Rd. Chen explained the situation and their actions, and they were praised for their bravery and quick thinking.

But as they began to debrief, the team began to realize just how far-reaching the consequences of their experiment could be. They had altered the timeline in a way that could have catastrophic effects, and they knew that they had to take responsibility for their actions.

The team spent weeks analysing the data they had collected and the events that had occurred during their experiment. They compiled a report outlining the risks and dangers of time travel, and they made recommendations for how to safely conduct experiments in the future.

One of their main recommendations was to only conduct experiments in controlled environments with extensive safety protocols in place. They also recommended that experiments be conducted with a smaller team of researchers to minimize the potential for mistakes. They stressed the importance of understanding the full consequences of any actions before making any jumps through time.

The report was presented to the government officials and was met with mixed reactions. Some officials were supportive of the team's efforts to prevent any more temporal paradoxes, while others were sceptical of the risks of time travel and were hesitant to support any further research.

Despite the mixed reactions, the team was determined to continue their work. They knew that the potential benefits of time travel were too great to ignore, but they also knew that they had to be careful. They continued to conduct experiments in a controlled environment, with strict safety protocols in place, and they made sure to carefully analyse the potential consequences of their actions before making any jumps through time.

As they continued their research, the team began to discover new and exciting applications for time travel. They were able to observe historical events first-hand, to study the origins of the universe, and to explore alternate timelines. They were making ground-breaking discoveries, and they knew that they were on the verge of something incredible.

But they also knew that with great power came great responsibility. They had seen the consequences of time travel first-hand, and they knew that they had to be careful with their newfound abilities. They continued to work tirelessly, always striving to make sure that they understood the full implications of their actions before making any jumps through time.

In the end, the team's research helped to pave the way for a new era of discovery and exploration. They had unlocked the secrets of time travel, but they had also learned a valuable lesson about the importance of responsibility and caution. The team's story would go down in history as a cautionary tale of the dangers of time travel, but it would also be remembered as a story of bravery, determination, and ground-breaking scientific discovery.

CHAPTER SIX

"A New Discovery"

The team had been working on their time travel experiments for several years, carefully refining their methods and taking every precaution to avoid any potential mishaps. They had made some incredible discoveries along the way, but they knew that there was still so much more to explore.

One day, as they were analysing their latest set of data, Rd. Reynolds noticed something unusual. There was a pattern in the data that they had never seen before, and it seemed to indicate that there was a gap in their knowledge of the universe. Intrigued, the team began to investigate.

As they delved deeper into the data, they realized that there was a region of the universe that they had never been able to observe directly. The region was too far away, too distant for their telescopes to capture any meaningful information. But the team knew that if they could somehow travel to that region, they could unlock some of the universe's greatest mysteries.

Excited by the possibility of a new discovery, the team began to pour all of their resources into developing a new, more advanced time travel machine. They worked tirelessly, pushing themselves to the brink of exhaustion as they attempted to create a device that could transport them farther than they had ever gone before.

Months passed, and the team worked around the clock, barely sleeping, eating, or taking breaks. But finally, they succeeded. They had created a new time travel machine that could transport them to the farthest reaches of the universe.

With trepidation and excitement, the team climbed into the machine and initiated the jump. The sensation was like nothing they had ever experienced before, a feeling of being stretched and compressed at the same time, as if their very atoms were being pulled apart and then put back together again.

When the jump was complete, the team found themselves in a strange, unfamiliar region of space. The stars were different, the colours were different, and the laws of physics seemed to be slightly altered. But they also realized that they were seeing something that no human being had ever seen before.

The team spent months exploring the region, gathering data, and making observations. They witnessed the birth of stars and the formation of galaxies, and they observed phenomena that they had only ever theorized about before. They were making discoveries that would change the course of human history.

But as they continued their work, the team began to realize that there was a danger to their discovery. They had seen the awesome power of the universe first-hand, and they knew that with that power came great responsibility. They knew that they had to be careful, and that they had to make sure that their discoveries were used for the betterment of humanity, rather than for personal gain.

The team returned to their own time, eager to share their findings with the world. But they also knew that they had to be cautious. They had to make sure that their discoveries were understood and appreciated, and that they were not misused or exploited for the wrong reasons.

The team spent years working on their research, presenting their findings to the scientific community, and pushing the boundaries of what was possible. They had made some of the greatest discoveries in human history, but they also knew that they had a duty to use their knowledge for the greater good.

In the end, the team's work helped to transform the way that humans understood the universe. They had unlocked secrets that had been hidden for billions of years, and they had opened new possibilities for exploration and discovery. And they had done it all with a sense of responsibility and caution, knowing that the power of their discoveries could be both awe-inspiring and dangerous.

CHAPTER SEVEN

"The Time Travellers' Dilemma"

As the years passed, the team's discoveries continued to shape the course of human history. New technologies emerged, new theories were formulated, and the world moved forward with a renewed sense of awe and curiosity about the universe.

But even as they celebrated their successes, the team knew that they were facing a difficult challenge. Time travel was still a largely uncharted territory, and they were discovering new questions and dilemmas at every turn.

One of the biggest dilemmas facing the team was the question of how to handle knowledge of the future. They had seen first-hand how their actions in the past could have unexpected consequences on the future, and they knew that their discoveries could change the course of history.

At first, the team was careful to keep their knowledge of the future to themselves. They didn't want to interfere with the natural course of events, or to risk causing unintended harm. But as they continued to travel through time, they began to realize that the distinction between past, present, and future was not as clear-cut as they had once thought.

In one of their trips, they discovered a critical event that would take place in the future. They were faced with a difficult decision: should they intervene, and try to prevent the event from happening, or should they stay out of it and allow events to unfold naturally?

The team debated the issue for weeks, but they ultimately decided that they could not sit by and let tragedy occur. They knew that they had the power to make a difference, and they felt a moral obligation to use that power for good.

So, they jumped to the future, and worked tirelessly to prevent the tragedy from happening. It was not an easy task, and they faced many obstacles and challenges along the way. But in the end, they were successful, and they returned to their own time feeling proud of what they had accomplished.

However, their actions did not go unnoticed. As news of the team's success spread, they began to receive criticism from some who felt that they had overstepped their bounds. People were worried that their actions had disrupted the natural course of events, and that the future would be irreversibly altered as a result.

The team was torn. On the one hand, they were proud of what they had accomplished. They had saved lives, and they had made the world a better place. But on the other hand, they knew that their actions could have unintended consequences, and that the future was now more uncertain than ever before.

In the end, the team realized that they were facing a moral dilemma. They had to balance their desire to do good with their responsibility to respect the natural order of events. They knew that they could not undo what they had already done, but they could make a commitment to be more careful in the future.

The team redoubled their efforts to understand the consequences of their actions, and they developed new protocols to ensure that they were not interfering with events in a way that would have unintended consequences. They continued to make discoveries and push the boundaries of what was possible, but they did so with a newfound sense of caution and responsibility.

In the end, the team realized that they were on a journey of discovery that would never truly end. There would always be new questions to answer, new dilemmas to face, and new discoveries to make. But they also knew that they were part of a legacy, a group of people who had dared to dream big and push the boundaries of what was possible. And they felt a deep sense of pride and responsibility to continue that legacy, for the betterment of all humanity.

CHAPTER EIGHT

"The Ultimate Discovery"

Years had passed since the team had first set out on their journey, and they had accomplished many amazing things. They had discovered new technologies, solved countless mysteries of the universe, and even helped to prevent tragedy in the future. But there was one discovery that had always eluded them, one mystery that they had been unable to solve.

That mystery was the nature of the universe itself. Despite all their knowledge and all their discoveries, the team still didn't understand the fundamental nature of the universe. They knew that there were laws and principles that governed everything around them, but they didn't know why those laws existed or where they came from.

For years, the team had searched for answers, studying the behaviour of particles and exploring the farthest reaches of space. But no matter how far they went or how much they discovered, they always seemed to be just out of reach of the ultimate answer.

It wasn't until a chance encounter with a group of advanced beings that the team finally began to glimpse the true nature of the universe. The beings, who had evolved to a state far beyond humanity, had discovered the fundamental principles of the universe, and they were willing to share their knowledge with the team.

Over the course of several months, the team worked with the beings to understand the universe in a way that they had never thought possible. They learned about the origins of the universe, the underlying principles that governed its behaviour, and the secrets of its fate.

It was a revelation unlike any other. The team had always known that the universe was vast and complex, but now they understood just how magnificent it truly was. They saw the universe as a vast and interconnected network, governed by principles that were at once simple and profound.

But with this new understanding came a new set of questions and dilemmas. The team realized that the universe was not a static entity, but one that was constantly changing and evolving. And they wondered how their newfound knowledge would impact the future.

They debated for months, trying to understand the full implications of their discovery. They knew that their knowledge could be used for good or for ill, and they wanted to make sure that it was used in the right way.

In the end, the team decided to share their knowledge with the world. They knew that it would be a transformative discovery, one that would change the way that humanity viewed the universe forever. And they hoped that by sharing their knowledge, they could help to inspire future generations to continue the journey of discovery that they had started.

And so, the team published their findings, sharing their knowledge with the world. It was a momentous occasion, and the world was changed forever. People began to see the universe in a new light, and they were inspired to explore and discover in ways that they had never thought possible.

The team knew that their work was far from over. There would always be new discoveries to make, new questions to answer, and new dilemmas to face. But they also knew that they had contributed to the greater good, one that would be remembered for generations to come.

As they looked back on their journey, the team felt a sense of awe and wonder at all that they had accomplished. They had pushed the boundaries of what was possible, and they had discovered secrets that had been hidden for millennia. And they knew that their journey had only just begun.

CHAPTER NINE

"The Price of Knowledge"

As the world grappled with the revelations of the team's ultimate discovery, there were those who saw it as an opportunity to exploit the newfound knowledge for their own gain.

Governments and corporations around the world began to invest heavily in research and development, hoping to harness the power of the universe for their own purposes. They saw the potential for new technologies, new weapons, and new forms of energy, and they were determined to be the ones to unlock it.

But as the pace of discovery increased, so too did the risks. The laws of the universe were not to be trifled with, and the consequences of meddling with them could be catastrophic.

The team watched with growing concern as governments and corporations engaged in increasingly risky experiments, pushing the boundaries of what was safe and ethical. They knew that it was only a matter of time before something went terribly wrong.

And then it did.

A lab in Asia had been experimenting with a new form of energy, one that promised to revolutionize the world. But the experiment went awry, and the energy began to spiral out of control. It was a catastrophic failure, and the resulting explosion decimated the surrounding area.

The team was stunned by the magnitude of the disaster. They had always known that there were risks to exploring the unknown, but they never imagined that the consequences could be so severe.

The incident sparked a global debate about the risks and rewards of scientific discovery. Many argued that the pursuit of knowledge was worth any price, that the benefits far outweighed the risks. Others pointed to the dangers of unchecked exploration and called for greater oversight and regulation.

The team found themselves at the centre of the debate. They had been the ones to unlock the secrets of the universe, and they felt a sense of responsibility for the consequences of that discovery.

They knew that the pursuit of knowledge was not without risk, but they also knew that the rewards were too great to ignore. They believed that the key to success was not in limiting exploration, but in ensuring that it was done safely and responsibly.

And so, the team decided. They would work with governments and corporations around the world to develop a set of guidelines and regulations for scientific research. They would use their knowledge to help ensure that the pursuit of knowledge was done in a way that was safe, ethical, and responsible.

It was a difficult and complex task, but the team was committed to making it work. They worked tirelessly, traveling the world and meeting with leaders in science, government, and industry. They spoke of the risks and rewards of scientific discovery, and they shared their knowledge and expertise to help guide the way forward.

It was a slow and difficult process, but eventually, the team began to see the results of their efforts. Governments and corporations around the world began to adopt the new regulations, and the risks of scientific research were greatly reduced.

The team knew that there would always be risks to exploration and discovery, but they also knew that the pursuit of knowledge was too important to ignore. And with their guidance and expertise, they believed that the world could continue to explore the unknown in a way that was safe, ethical, and responsible.

CHAPTER TEN

"The Legacy of Discovery"

Years had passed since the team had first unlocked the secrets of the universe. They had all gone their separate ways, pursuing their own interests and careers. But they remained united by the experience they had shared, and by the knowledge that they had helped to shape the world in a meaningful way.

As they looked back on their discovery, they marvelled at the impact it had had on the world. New technologies had been developed, new forms of energy had been harnessed, and new opportunities had been created. The world had been transformed in ways that they could never have imagined.

But they also recognized that the work was far from done. The universe was still full of mysteries, and there were still countless discoveries to be made. And with each new discovery came new opportunities and new challenges.

The team knew that their legacy was not just in the discoveries they had made, but in the way they had approached their work. They had shown that the pursuit of knowledge could be done in a way that was safe, ethical, and responsible. They had demonstrated that the risks of exploration could be mitigated, and that the rewards were worth the effort.

And so, they continued to work in their own fields, always pushing the boundaries of what was known and what was possible. They knew that their work was just a small part of a much larger effort, but they also knew that every step forward brought the world closer to a greater understanding of the universe.

Years turned into decades, and the team began to pass the torch to a new generation of scientists and explorers. They watched with pride as these new scientists continued to push the boundaries of what was known, building on the work that they had started.

And as they looked back on their long and storied careers, the team knew that they had made a difference in the world. They had helped to shape the way that scientific discovery was done, and they had opened up new possibilities for future generations.

Their legacy was not just in the discoveries they had made, but in the way they had approached their work. They had shown that the pursuit of knowledge could be done in a way that was safe, ethical, and responsible. And in doing so, they had helped to make the world a better and more interesting place.

9 798889 860839

Printed by Libri Plureos GmbH in Hamburg, Germany